VISIONS OF A
TREMULOUS MAN

ALSO BY VINCENZO BILOF

The Violators (forthcoming)
Dark Rising
Japanese Werewolf Apocalypse
Nightmare of the Dead
The Horror Show
Mother, I'm Not an Android (I Promise)
Confessions of the Impaler
Gravity Comics Massacre
Vampire Strippers from Saturn
Vincenzo Bilof Must Die

The Zombie Ascension Series:
Necropolis Now
Queen of the Dead
Saint Pain

VISIONS OF A
TREMULOUS MAN

Vincenzo Bilof

illustrated by
Jim Agpalza

WEIRDO **C**~MAGNET

Visions of a Tremulous Man
by Vincenzo Bilof

First published in 2015 by
WEIRDO **C̃** MAGNET
an imprint of Leaky Boot Press
http://www.leakyboot.com

ISBN: 978-1-909849-20-4

Contents

PROLOGUE

I

Cracking months devour flowers
child scream wallpaper coefficients
Left knuckle breathes,
kerrack
kerrack
they asked him why his face was a pancake
they asked him why his garden burned
secrets beneath ice cream caravans
box full of tiny eyes
"hello, this is Walter, please leave a message"
and there is no message.

II

Released into the wild exposition
"I belive in God, and I know I can be a good man"
It is our unanimous decision parole
be granted

UNTO ME

a parole officer will be assigned
there are still pending investigations

"I love my wife, and every day
I want... sorry... I hate crying like this..."

that's okay, Walter
the letters you've written to that girl's
family over the years have made a difference
I think we can all learn from you
forgiveness is a powerful thing

"she's married now, got a little boy"

around
—of—
laughter

people have the power to heal
live their lives
"I carry the guilt upon my soul"
Walter, you have been an inspiration
teaching others to follow
your example
"I was a lonely man, I had low self-esteem
and I never wanted to hurt
anybody
I just... know... that sexual deviancy
is an illness
and God..."

III

Everyone knows the woman
cutting her lawn
bag filled with clippings,
details of her life so nothing, so nothing
the husband molested a girl

oh they don't know but if they did

everyone knows the woman
cutting her lawn
lips sealed by secrets
they think it is guilt and shame lonely woman
the husband molested

the brother looks after her such a damaged
but we do not
her fault for marrying a
pretty if she wore makeup

everyone
peered through their windows
FUCKING MOVE OUT OF OUR
NEIGHBORHOOD
TAKE THAT SICK MAN WITH YOU
AND YOU'RE SICK
WHY DIDN'T YOU DIVORCE HIM

processional, heroic,
silent

IV

complete the following sentences in cruciform
tentacle wires, veins, open wide your face
rocket ships melt on Mars in reverse
If, you know, if

They found him

BIG IF
she'll wear an apron on fantasy holiday festivals
black nest of curls and a mask,

can this metaphor surrender
wooden spoon murders

hard-boiled eggs on the burner
Sigourney Weaver cliffs and maps
scimitar cuts mouth corners

this is not where he'll hide
but she carries rubber souls
into the shower
her face cracks the quiet

and he wants to go back to concrete walls
cold iron, cold world, cell full
of confessional

V

(clatter)

"We haven't fucked in several hours, counting to ten plus a thousand, it feels like."
Nobody is listening to him, and that is something.
Curtain fabric between two fingers, shaking.

"Maybe she'll be home before dinner."

Summer storm gray afternoon. There isn't a storm. Humidity succubus parabolas
speak:
"Nabokov you asshole." The comment is random. A stranger who shows up to a hockey game, a stranger who cannot find their seat, a stranger who finds a seat, a stranger who does not feel comfortable in the seat they have found because it does not belong to them, they do not own the seat, ownership is implied with the purchase of a ticket, and this stranger is haunted, troubled, paranoid, and leaves the game. The stranger does not know who won.

Usually quiet in this neighborhood, but they know. They know who sleeps inside the house. They. Know. They have found him on the computer. They have found his name. They have seen his face before. They have seen his face and he does not understand why he cannot repent. He cannot
repent
mostly because he wants to do it again. He doesn't want to but he does. It's not him. This is not the real him.
—Long legs behind a white trophy dog.
—Young hair made of gold.
—Oh. Oh. Lookee here. Lookee.

WALTER
(THE FREE MAN, THE URBAN SPRAWL)

I

Nobody has to hurt
tongue rolled teeth
lips soaked in tongue
teeth like buildings, skyscrapers
I don't look into your eyes but your mouth
I can see it, the girl
pieces of me bled into those girls
pieces of me bled in prison
I could see shards in porcelain
cell block cracks, cold iron
mirror is full of you
even in showers of pain
swallowing
mouthful of water against the tile
pushing me, pushing me,
Scarlet was the second girl's name wasn't it
pushing me, pushing me.

II

Those years I killed
Laughter filling streets
Billboards speak alien
Those clouds, a cumulus

III

(In a park full of rain I found her
Pictures of lightning)
now this man

Detective.
"You're meek. How did you
have your way with them?"

Leave me alone.

"I can't. You know I torment
you because
it's fun for me."

Fun for you.

"Reminding you that you're
a piece, I mean a real piece."

Real. This meek skin pales
in their eyes, rolling, disappearing

"Your wife has you wrapped."

My mother was dead by the time I was four.

"Read about it in your file."
Everything about a life on pages,
documented,
database-sorted
technology-snorted.

IV

Mr. Vegas is the Vivid Man. Not a dark man, but a vivid man. He walked into the room and cracked his neck. Belly bulging over his waistline. A belly pregnant with stomach. He looked the girl over and nodded. He appraised her.

I had hoped she was young enough. Perfect enough. I trained her. Practiced with her. Made sure she was ready for Mr. Vegas. If he is not satisfied, I will be destroyed. This is true. This is the solution

to me. I must perform my duties or I will be destroyed.

His fingers probed her. Inside her. Scooping my desire from inside. The milk of human longing and violence. Interior thighs shimmering, shiny, moist. Glistening perhaps. A good word. Glistening.

Mr. Vegas shoved his fingers into his mouth to make sure it was me. He knew what I tasted like. He licked his fingers clean. His fingers were always clean.

I did what I was supposed to do. The girl was ready for him. Trained.

V

When and how the apology
Hands made of glass, blown
Angel dust tears
How I have become this

Listen for the apology
You, me

There was college?
There was
A white house
Tell me about the white house

There was a boy?
A girl?
Tell me what they look like.

Your grades were good.
Which college?
Did you paint?
Track star. With those legs.

Ah, you can dream.
Behind your eyes only.

Thought about you today,
Or smile, you can
Smile. Let me taste your hate.
I've known it forever.
Your disgust is my friend.
My friend is in you, through
You.

I didn't want to hurt you
they made me do it

these are all the things

the ritual
these are all the things
I shared with them
all of them
each of them
all of them
things
these are the things
those were the things
the things
ritual

VI

We were stars, starlight
Swirling along the floor
A ship I found in the sky
Airship, float into
Computer space responses

Twitter twitter boil and tremble
The spots on your hands
Fingers folded in prayer form
Your gown spun

Orbital eyes revolving my irises
I found you, my treasure (you who would become

wife)

Upon this moon we dance
Twilight owls
envy your neckline

You haven't smiled since then
Sometimes I feel the smile
Or pretend I see it

Why can't we find the moon?

Wash your hands,
This kitchen, my haven,
Your sink, your hands,
Run the water for steam
I've heard the sound
Your hands make with soap

The girls you gave me
The girls I gave you
All for you,
"Out, out!"

I sit here in my spot
Wondering where the moon has gone.

VII

Prison is yesterday and so are these ghosts
I am backward and forward on nightmare-carrying boats
A plague upon my past, my future, my windows
I was programmed to make sure these girls would never become
widows

I am electric in variations of myself
My wife kidnapped them, a master of stealth
This design included my name for love
Conditional surrender to which prison
love
or
love
or
today

Dripping into
this picture window
ignore the wife
her brother
exist in phases of light

I shall not beg
not for death

VII

Now I will think about the girl
who walked her dog
like so many other girls
the first time, I will think about
the first time

Margaret the wife, whose eyes
were black behind her wedding veil
has told me only that Mr. Vegas
has work for us to continue

the work
the great work

blonde girl blonde girl
what do you see?

the first time
"you think I married you for love… some
delusion or another…"
"look at him Margie, how pitiful, weeping"
"you were picked, you were watched"
"vulnerable boy, Mama's boy"
"you're going to possess this girl, take her"
"cum inside of her blood, Walter"
"the only real love is the love I have for my
brother"
"your wife is mine, Walter"
"evisceration isn't so bad, but it's messy"
"what was the youngest?"
"I think we had one that was 9"
"oh, yeah. Margie, you have a damn good
memory"

my wife has the memory of lawns

overreaching weeds over brick
landscaping, trimmed

("there's grass on the field, Walter,
so let her eat your balls!")

I already knew she liked the tasteof cinnamon

IX

found an old love letter
*Margaret, do you, um, can you, I mean, read it over, see if, I
mean, you know*
what girls

like
*is this going to, um, oh, I can't, please, I don't want to hurt
anyone*
IF YOU LOVE

on the bed, she stirs
there was a cathedral in prison
the light was the same

—you got caught because you're weak
     letting the girl go
     she never saw our faces
     and you think
     I will love you
     because... heh, oh, heh heh heh,
     you hoped I changed
     and you knew Mr. Vegas
     would find you
     and you should know
     we continued our work
     with other men
     several men were inside me
     they all said the same thing
     how tight I am
     like I'm younger
     but none of them were as efficient
     as my Walter
     sleep
     I saw your eyes today—

she
love letter crumbled in
fingers, clenched
teeth
have permission to bleed

X

We were in my basement.
My brother in-law is a good man.
He
didn't wear a shirt, a wig on his chest and belly,
MR. LAS VEGAS
in the basement, hands on his belted hips, brown belt,
brown belt
WHAT DO YOU SEE? (a cute
song, isn't
)

"This is the one we wanted," he said.
Blood red hair. Pencil black skirt.
Lead-black.
Oh my blood flows. Seventeen.
My God seventeen,
she was.
Seventeen virginal
years or not.

"My sister is good, isn't she?" MR. VEGAS asked.
He he he he he.
Like Pokemon. She catches them all.

XI

This is what
you do
This is what you
be
now and then
pretty girls
I will bring them and you will
see, experience, feel
how tight,
how real
how feel you
I am an angel
say it
I am an angel
I was a movie star
I am an angel
I am your goddess

I HEARD YOUR NAME IN PRISON

You will hear my name
when we
are gone
apart.
You will see
me there, in the dark
and know
I am real
I am purse
Goddess or god, dark or
blight,

I WILL ALWAYS LISTEN TO YOU

You will always listen to me

these pretty girls
whispered
when you were with them
when you were them
these pretty girls
laughed
disgusting child
disgust me child

I WILL ALWAYS LOVE YOU

You will always love me
you will eat
your breakfast
you will eat
these girls
after you feed them
violate their physical
you will be

THE GIRLS ARE SO PRETTY EVEN WHEN THEY LAUGHED

the girls are so pretty even when they laughed
they laugh
until you cut
they laugh
until you hurt

I WILL HAVE REVENGE FOR US

you will have revenge for us

I WILL ENJOY MYSELF

you will enjoy myself

I WILL NOT FAIL YOU

YOU WILL NOT FORGIVE ME IF I FAIL

I WILL DO THIS

I AM THIS

XII

She won't look at me

The girl outside walks the
white neighborhood

tiny dog
on a leash

wife tells me dinner is ready
tiny dog
remember her
tomorrow's daydreams

I have seen a lot of white
in my time

XIII

The men who decided I was safe to live outside
recommended I keep pages
words to discover the pain
repression they said, repression
we are here for you
out there

so many bottles of cure
CALL THIS NUMBER FOR MORE REPRESSION
sedative darkness numb, numb

we know you can function like everybody else
we know you can live like everybody else
you're a good man

Unencumbered into this vast garage of skulls
in the middle of the desert

you burned that place down
symbiosis of identity, conclusions upon conclusions

you didn't listen to their father
there is truth in happiness, too,
some kind of divinity

but I have slept in the color black

shall this disease spread with a glance
you have talked about televisions glowing in a thunderstorm

let me walk into the world again a free man
to talk again to strangers
practice by composing love letters my wife shall never read
one day you will share one with her
and you will discover that she loves you

(I still remember the day
I was asked why I would never
divorce her)

Entry 1

I don't think this is a journal. A good researcher keeps some kind of record. Maybe I should just say it aloud and record it. I kind of like writing it. I feel like I have the opportunity of a lifetime. This will be a breakthrough of modern psychology if my theories are correct.

Here are my goals/theories/plans for my own sake, because once I start, I can't back down. I'm putting my life in danger.

Walter has just been released from prison after several years of incarceration. I have some of the public documents regarding the case. He sexually assaulted a teenage girl, but the pending charges and investigations that have not yet been closed are going to haunt him. There was an uproar in a town hall meeting over it. People are upset he's coming to live here.

Walter's name has been mentioned in connection with several disappearances of young girls, and the missing girls have a few things in common, which should have been obvious.

The girls are from impoverished families.
The girls have long legs.
The girls live/lived in major metropolitan cities.

These facts lead me to believe that the girls were carefully selected. Why couldn't enough evidence be dredged up against him? Especially considering that his wife, Margaret, and her brother (can't remember his name off the top of my head and I'm too lazy to look) are related to a man who is now institutionalized. The brother was also brought up on charges of sexual assault and dishonorably discharged when he was in the military. Why didn't the cases get reopened?

I don't want this to become a social or political commentary. I have to keep my goals in mind.

I believe there is a strong connection between Margaret, her brother, and their father. I believe Walter was somehow coerced into violence. I think he is a helpless person, and his lack of self-esteem made him easy to manipulate.

So I will befriend him. I will make attempts to get to know him. I want to understand him. I want to help him. Then, I want to learn everything I can about his family. I believe they are sociopaths. But to what extent? How far does it go back? The father is certainly unique, and nobody put together the fact that their mother was murdered at a water park—the killer was never found—and the rest of the family was there!

Sociopathy, like many mental disorders, could be hereditary. If that is not true, then I can assume the father's masterful sociopathic tendencies could introduce us to an entirely new level of understanding about the condition, considering how calculated and perverse one must be to transform one's own family—and later, an innocent man—into murderers. It's almost like the father "converted" his children in cult-like fashion.

I see a lot of parallels to historic murder cases. I think a lot of missing girls and families await justice.

—Becca

DETECTIVE
(FRESH MONSTERS OF LUCID AQUARIUM)

I

Nobody nags, ha ha ha,
Pig pen, little Piggy
Television glow, projection tube,
they call it
Maybe I should get up, go to work,
Make phone calls. Drink
A
Beer. Check
The list. My list.

I'll watch cigar smoke scar my home
If I still had a wife,
Thoughts. No. What.
Maybe call. New person on the list.
His name?
If I don't know a name
There isn't a name, there isn't a name

A face, a crime,
a face, a victim.
Maybe victims. Victims?

Where's my cape and haircut?
They haven't fit
since my first day on the job.

II

Manilla dreams folder folded paper.
This is the one. Accused of murder, predator
Sexual predator. Call him? Call? Married,
Still married. Forgiveness? Guilt?

What terror holds a marriage together,
From cell block to home,
Where's my wife? Manslaughtered
Our years, happy anniversary
If I had been there.

The picture again. Sexual predator
Breathing suburban air, trees
And Halloween, kids riding their bikes
Here he is, here is and they know.

      She said "I do"
Means she would, she will
Means she'll be there,
Forgiving my street smell, blood sleeves,
Smeared makeup from teary-eyed girls
Knuckles, they get old, crumble
Hurt. Hurt.
      She didn't say goodbye,
I feel like a desert without sand,
An oasis without wind. I am still.
Every day is frightening because there are more, more, more
Of these manila folder marriages,
Long-legged teenagers damaged,
Some maybe killed.
They never got him on the murder charge.

III

Are you standing by a window?

"I'm your parole officer."

Are you a changed man?

"When I call, your ass picks up the phone. When I show up at you house, your ass is there. I'll be in internet chatrooms. Message boards. I'll be a little girl. I'll be sixteen. I'll get you. If you're still a sick fuck, I'll get you."

I am everywhere.

"Are there any questions?"

Your wife forgave you.

"You like blondes or brunettes? Your mommy abuse you? Your wife kick you around? Huh? Why don't you answer? Your wife kicks your around, doesn't she. Slaps you around. Calls you a bitch. You were a bitch in prison, I bet. They love sex offenders. I know they do. They know how much you want it."

This story was written yesterday.

"Say something."

Talk to me.

"If you so much as jerk off to porn, any porn, your ass is back in. You think those girls are all eighteen? You know they're not. I can track you. Your life isn't private. Your life is mine."

Talk.

IV

Lucid cloud cover
Robins chanting, parked cars
Medieval silence
Children hide behind these doors
Suburban monster haunts

V

There is laughter and sunlight and gold stars. The stars are gold and I want to watch sunsets because I am young and alive, but I am not. I am not young and maybe I am not alive. I am not who I was and I don't know who I will be but I know what I do. I know what I do and that is sometimes not me. That is not enough for me. Charlene. Chari. Charlene. Chari. I could try internet dating sites. MATCH.COM. I could look for her. A likeness of her. Is there a better version of the love I once had?

All my fault. This should be fun. I've never been here before. Took time off to feel sorry for myself. To wallow. To drink. To be a burn-out. To fade into flame. Cold flame.

Try waking up and realizing your life is dead. Your life is gone. The house stands but it's a skeleton. It's not who you remember. It's not what it used to feel like. I have woken up today and I have purpose, but it's the same purpose I had before only now I am in love. I know I am in love. This is my love affair and I will not stop loving.

Of course I am obsessed. I will not deny I am obsessed. I can't stop thinking about him. I can't stop thinking about what he has done, and what he might do. I want to catch him again. I want revenge against the world. I know my debilitations. Is that good? Is that enough? I know who I am. I don't need medications or doctors to tell me about the lingering psychosis. This psychosis does not linger.

VI

Watch the door swing wide.
Oh those blinking eyes.

This form I shape.

(you are
Feeling
Me
Eyes)

She is wearing a robe. Disability checks her.
Sizzle. Steam. Grease.
Take me inside.

We shall imprison each other in the eyes of the law.
We shall rape our souls with the best intentions.
We shall discard our intentions.

For some

Reason
I glance at my wedding ring. I forgot I wore it
Today.

VII

"Does she have to be in the room?"

The chess metaphor screams.
"My wife, Margaret. Meet Officer _____"

(Latin word for silence)
Silence

There, rewards us
"Are you going to stand there and continue to be an asshole?
You can have breakfast. You can relax. Sit down at least. Civility
is not dead."

My knight in shining armor
Wear your uniform tonight
When will you be home?
I've decided to leave you

"You raped underage girls. Tell me something else about
civility."

In manila words, they didn't get him for murder.
"I'm a free man. I've learned my lesson."

He forgot to deny GIRLS
You've changed
You're never home
You think you can change
... ...these people

"You bought them ice cream. Such a nice man. Stay off the
streets if you know what's good for you. Stay in your house.
These people know who you are. Your name is everywhere.
They know you. They will never forget you. Their kids will brag
about you. They live near a criminal. They have a criminal in
their neighborhood."

Stomach acid corrosion eatery

The wife is a monument
Her face is Andrew Jackson and maybe
The bust of Socrates, aged, dust face of Sphinx

Walter cracks his knuckles
Again, he cracks them.

The air here is stale. The air here does not have a smell
But all smells, all here. Dead bodies beneath my feet.
Dead bodies in dirt. Dead bodies are dirt.
People are not bodies. The creed.
PEOPLE ARE NOT BODIES.
And I am not here for them.

Don't turn around.
Stare back.
The wife is a crowbar.

I want to go out tonight
But I don't remember you.

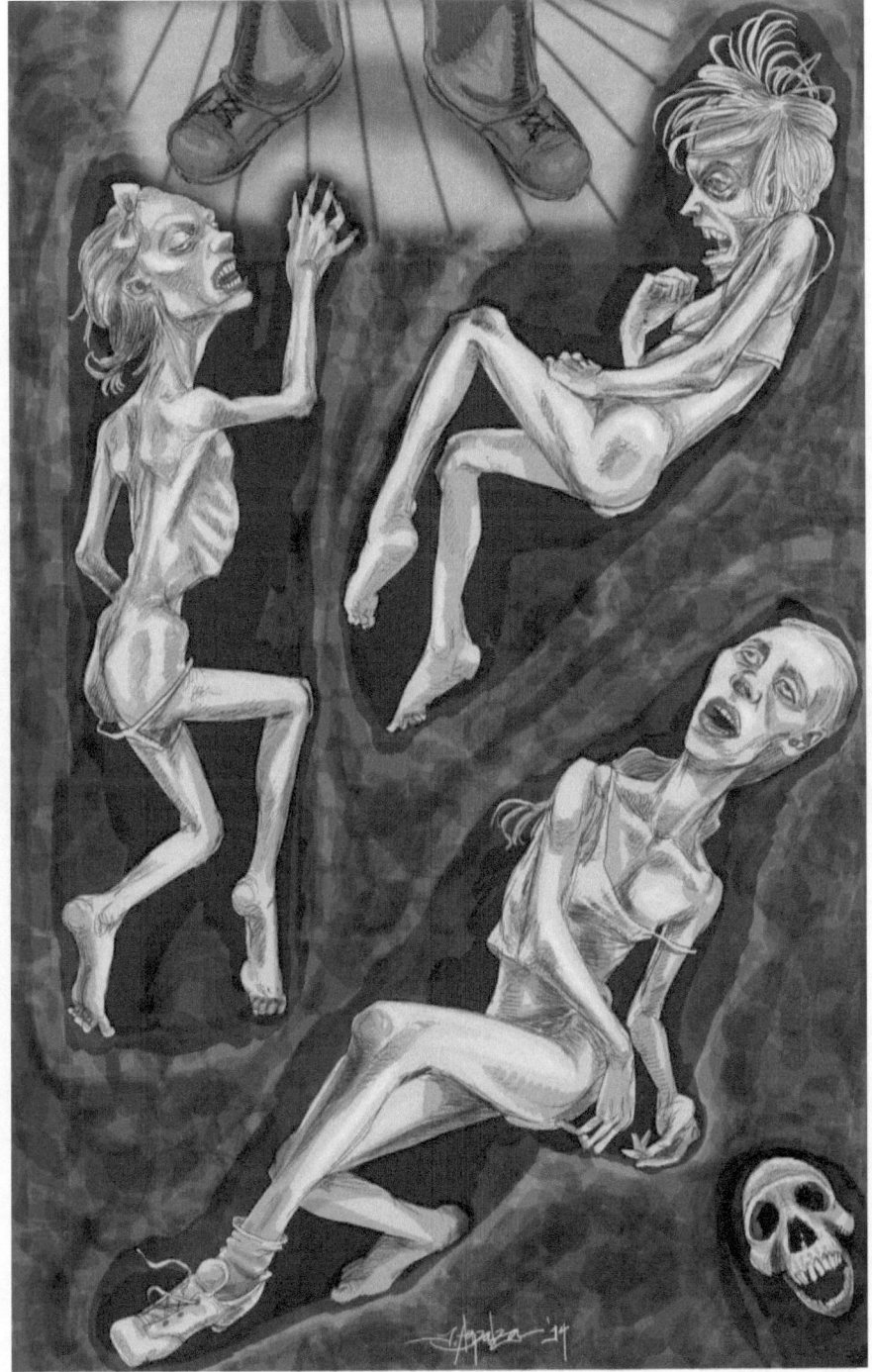

VIII

This is not my face today
Come to me tenderly
You wouldn't know love in young arms
You want your father like every good girl
I need to know him, to know you, to know him
Where have I? To know him again.

My wife thought children were cute
who will rock them to sleep
dear I don't know when I will be home
(girls spread out on the pavement like angels
pretty angels)
Overdosed on attention, boys and girls
Their parents, what were they
God my thoughts
Baby, baby,
Babies in cradles become angels
Babies become headlines
No, please dearest

This girl is someone's daughter
In the name of my mind
I've thought about her
Her, my face,
Plastered against glass,
Eyes focused on her wonder
That is wind

I'm sure the young man will protect you
In his dreams
Wet you,
So many paper angels
Illustrated chalk angels
black and white angels

Yesterday I saw a crib on a curb
Garbage day

IX

I can count all the years I have killed thoughts of flesh
The former wife would awake to empty mornings
In the name of law and order I did what was best
Among all the street queens this young girl is among lordlings

Text your boyfriend oh muse, I watch your fingers play
Language barrier of decades but I know how soft you are
Firm paradise I understand why I have joined the fray
You can be, you can be, oh yes, you can be my lucky star

Your head can whip from side to side with taped mouth
A hunter is brave and captures hearts and smiles
When you open your eyes through tears you'll love my house
The look I'll share I've seen in dozens of trials

A good police officer has justice as his goal
When I take your purity I will save your soul

X

I come from a town that has two funeral homes
and one church.
The landfill is overflowing

dead bicycles.
"Have you seen me?"
Mr. Gatsby asked.

XI

Brain shelves, shelved
In plastic bags these killers
Guess their names, guess them,
Whose pulsate stratagems
Sunken plastic bags, vacuum sucked
sealed, here on shelves
I hate starting the day with a dream

An empty space in
the Ziplock museum
the one I want and need,
the one I need and need and need

I don't want to be here anymore I guess
(I am not here)
I don't want be here anymore I guess
(I'm not here)

Bobby Fischer couldn't imagine
the nightmares they have, all of them
now mine, how predictable
haunted homicide man, haunted
homicide man
wake up and eat your breakfast.

XII

Twelve years in the kitchen
We didn't like that film
together, kitchen
I like this morning because the sun
just a little, though it has become much
turns blonde hair to red, radiant blood light
touching her hair, my wife's face carved
in desert broken hollows

"They lost again," I said
to paraphrase
SPORTS FAN perceptions

Bacon grease, crackling, smoking
Eggs
(*A Raisin the Sun,* read it in school, wondering
about chess books at home, the ones I wanted

to read, failure, this failure, another failure)

Bacon response, I move
Hands on her hips, the least I can do
the brain would slip a knife into the small
of her back and feel the blood on his fingers
maybe rub his fingertips together,
looking at the fingers not the corpse
not the corpse which slips to the floor,
I have always played this opponent
the invisible man, the present man

"One more week," she said.
The countdown to death.
You'd call it retirement,
with a touch of morning.

XIII

Moving pieces

Crime scene photgraphs
Black and white victim

Walter connected with disappearances
never charged
never tried

there's another man in the house
(they call him Mr. Vegas)
war veteran
Walter's... brother in law... lives
in the house
has lived there...

for a time

the case was solved ages ago
here I am

Moving pieces
a dead girl
used to be a baby
was held, swaddled,
fed, laughed, cried

what do these sick people
the father
murder trial
institution
Walter tried for sexual assault

of a minor

moving
pieces
Walter has not been to therapy

(Icarus)—has fallen asleep

his voice on the phone
muffled, distant panic
no man is cured without
the court of law's permission

moving pieecs
into bottles that have disappeared
here I am

the strategem is file-corrupt
folded into a neat history

I am moving my pieces
motion through brick
layers, atrocity, layers
empty houses

Entry 4

I have a feeling the detective is in over his head. There's enough documentation that's easy to find. More than anything, I worry that he will make things worse. I am concerned that the toxic environment will have an impact on him as it did Walter. I will record observations about him, too.

My work is not an unhealthy obsession, and I am "mature enough" to handle the work. Blood and murder are simply pieces of evidence belonging to victims. The victims have an identity, the blood and the pieces are just evidence used to conduct investigations.

I have conclued before that those who are interested in learning about sociopathy and pursuing it as a field of study must also have sociopathic tendencies. I do not look for consequences, but rather, an end result. The methods I use to conduct my research do not make me sociopathic, unless another person might otherwise research my own motivations, of which I am all-too aware.

My lack of experience shows up in my records. I tend to ramble. I wonder how bad it would be if I recorded myself speaking.

Walter continues to watch me from behind the living room window. He knows the time I will walk my dog. I do not see the brother inside the house often—he is more of shadow than a person with a face. Margaret's erratic behavior continues, and I feel this is the sticking point that I must figure out to puzzle through everything. She's watching a lot of television, mostly war movies and Christian sermons. She paces the house. She talks with Walter often, but there is no body-language indicators identify empathic or argumentative conversation. She has not mowed the lawn since Walter returned. The detective told Walter he would do it himself because he was worried that he wouldn't be able to see into the house beyond the weeds.

—Becca

MARGARET
(MOVIE THEATER STATIONS)

I

The garden is not important
(the girl's thighs are wet, sweaty)
I can see that
(she's a tease. Teases the boys at school)
Flannel, cowboy hat, black bra revelation
(do you know how she dreams at night)

In the cold iron bars I saw your face,
Not this one.
In the silence I heard your voice.
In the dark I thought of you.
Creator, God, reformer.

(This is the one we like)
Herald of tradition
Snakeskin neckline
Springtime trespasser
I vowed to break your father's rules.
(You will bring her to us).

III

I will tell you about my father
but only because
I am the only one

who knows or understands. I
am, myself,
involved from the beginning. The world is a dangerous

place
teach these young people how to walk upright
if they don't learn they cannot live
if they cannot learn they cannot learn to live
if they must die they should die
not in the name of God or species
for the sake of ourselves because we can,

we can
cull them

even my brother can speak to sirens
droplets of ice stuck between his teeth
the boys and the girls must be taught pain but where
has it gone
this pain we understand and hear
I can save demons with gentle kisses
in the fires of a burning Rome
look there for tyrants, look there
statues evoke messianic temple disease
the flaccid path

walk the flaccid path

Robert Frost was taught to us in school
I thought of the flaccid path for my father
because my mother was not worthy. she was sick and she did not
understand. this

—sickness was ignorance—
at a water park, shriveled, a century old among the immortals
sparkle water sunshine falls,
in line, we wait,
waited.
waiting still

don't listen to your father he is mad.
I'm sorry for what he has done to you. It didn't have to be this
way. I have infected us. I believed in his eyes but there is no
throat to hide the flies.

My brother coughed
enjoy this treat

line moving, forward
someone else in the place we used to stand
I know what you're thinking
he's a saint but what he has done to you is wrong
where was our father that day?

III

Ambulance screams
Olympic marathon escape
children hustling, carried, crying
What? They don't know. What?

I don't see Mother anywhere
Would she look by the farm animals for us
Dad's car, he's here
We are inside,
brother, sister, father,
FATHER

Driving away, almost parked
in waves of people, crashing
over metal, sunlight-soaked concrete
the water park sign is like a church bell
that cannot make a sound

No voices inside of the car
thought frozen.
Index finger poised over his moustache,
FATHER drives.

"What's happening?" Brave Sir Brother
has asked for a word.
We had to leave.
There was a murder at the water park.
Father would show us pictures

when we came home
of our mother.

IV

It is the sound of thunder
without noise.

I sat on his lap.
"She was pretty."
A public bathroom painted red.
Not paint.
Ketchup.
Not ketchup.
"I never loved her more. Look at how pretty."
A rat on the floor, eatching the ketchup
that isn't ketchup.

Not a rat.
Meat, like chicken or ravioli,
ravioli isn't meat
chicken that looks like ravioli,
ravioli-colored meat.

It is the sound of thunder. Rushing
toward ear canals,
flooding.

His hands were big
not trembling with pictures
knuckles, everywhere.

"I made sure the police knew."
It was the right thing to do,
of course.
"A human is beautiful
at birth?"

There was nodding.
A sound like.

"How wasteful

if we cannot be turned inside
out. See everything we cannot see,
feel nothing when we can feel everything
at the end. Silence is not
for us."

Mother did not have a funeral.
They did not find her killer.

Practice
mates

perfect
we are so perfect

My brother's body belongs
to a man, hair,
in the dark

I can say this now
His name wasn't always
a city

He lay on the bed
"You must learn how to love."
FATHER
had these words.

Scarred my eyes with flesh
Mysteries of the body
This is us,
the skin in the dark

Vaseline wooden spoon
Window open
Only a crack
Not even a breeze
No curtains stir

Bedsheet rustle through history
wet fire between parts of me
My brother,
for my father.

V

Glass shadows slapped across
basementdark

Countries of thigh
swinginglamp

Masks are for the weak
altersacrifice

We do not understand masks
whimperingeyes

Look how wide everything really is
blackstainsonstone

This is not an experiment
insideofher

They do not have faces anymore
memoriesdrown

Victims syphoned by acid barrels
skulls,
apples, upon the surface

VI

Walter husband mows the lawn
his glances trace
castle
            maiden

how do I
reprieve emotion-cast
from this tower
noise inside of another bedroom

tomorrow there will be rain
            windowpane autograph

idle spirit dust
me

sighs the windscape

                        on another planet, clad in entropy
his head
misses her glance

wrists chaff
            those are my severed limbs in a garbage bag

VII

All I did was watch
HA yes HA yes
I was the practice

> pliers
> wet stains
> inside of cellars
> tombs
> mold-corruption of dark

My brother was inside of me
FATHER said
the plan for humanity
the plan

> if I understood the concept
> of theoretical apologies
> *I would not have married your mother*
> *would have stolen my children*
> *but I have cut throats*
> *the temptation*

YES BROTHER
ha, all I did was watch

how many girls committed to the knife
this is not yesterday,
but an accounting for the melting trees

my eyes list to the right
hours decide against blinking

> *human sacrifice is the oldest*
> *form of love*
> *worship-testimonial*
> *we do not undersand sympathy*
> *invented to placate*

we shall not have a license
for freedom's wings

inside me, everything fills
reaching for dead children
I am the waking imbalance
the syphon
the calligraphy of a postscript
a mortuary descendant

a woman
trapped in a page

VIII

there is a force behind my eyes... "all flesh sings for the aptitude"... records tremble against fractures imaginary or otherwise... a casette deck with a tape that is mostly air... the button impressed... hiss of zero... long hiss of zero... "it's time to go back"... repeated... "it's time to go back..." a detective watches from his hilltop vestial glasscape infanticide eyes, gaze attached to wonder and anticipation... "it's time to go back"... if I hide beneath my bed the dead girls will question their sanity... "it's time"... this movement of wandering is clasped 'tween fingernails... "it's time to go back"... check email for skeletons... there are no vapor trails where my husband sleeps... "it's time to go back..." the detective asked why my brother lives here, why he is called Mr. Vegas... long hiss speak to a termiminus... all cities are filled with the light of murdered angels... the cosmopolitan hiss...

IX

Basements remember
Faces of cauldrons melted
The houses we knew
Victims don't require names
anymore
Tunnel mind, tunnel of mine

X

I am sorry for the mess on the floor
It is not an occult symbol
I have worked so hard for this carpet
and I am not sad
nail polish has painted the fibers
purple
while I live in a colorless realm

"this gets interesting when you're upset"
confusion, not delirium
Walter's return has touched my spinal
my brother is not my husband
I am the concubine of horror
I am the succubus of shards

"one of your phases. I am getting pizza and beer."
I live inside the wallpaper
there is something classical
depression, inertia,
long stretches of pause

this is your exit
on my knees among the stains
of broken color, clown tragedy

Entry 5

I have seen the brother. He looks like his father. Whenever I look at his name, and try to remember his name, I find myself forgetting it shortly after.

It has been some time since my last entry. Walter and I exchange waves now, because he is often out mowing his lawn while I am walking Pansie, my dog. I think it is perfectly normal for someone to forget to mention an animal's name. I didn't think it was important, but now I have included it, for my own purposes.

It is not difficult to keep my thoughts in order, but there is a lot to think about. My grades in school are good because they must be good. I am not distracted at school. At night, I am reading Helter Skelter *for the third time. I don't think the book is providing any additional insight into my theories, and I will stop reading it. I shouldn't have recorded here that I am reading it again, although the fact that it was not helpful may be a useful reminder in the future.*

Things have progressed slowly. There are times I wonder if I should give up. I know that once Walter talks with me once, that he has talked himself into talking to me, and he perhaps will want me to save him, rescue him from the household. I think redemption and Heaven are on his mind.

Margaret spends most of her time in the basement, now.

—Becca

MR. VEGAS
(SHOWMANSHIP, OBELISKS)

I

Off to war and the sister
Wasn't forgotten. No.
Spectral veil in Kuwait,
the desert planet
My first moment in a church.

Father didn't approve,
I had to leave. Had to.
What I learned.

Helicopters vibrating sky
Where a church does not have a roof
Pillars of flame,
Everything is smoke and prayer
The stones were old, the guns were silent

The guns were silent
In brothels that smelled like jasmine
And dying freshwater fish,
A place where my skills were found.

My advice: be brave, young soldier
Do you have a sister?
These eyelashes are years
Remember that roofless church
And the thunder drowning voices?

For many men, it was their first time.
I picked for them.
The youngest for me. The youngest
Who were sisters.

Spread them out like cards
flip them over
ha ha ha
the best advice I had
to trade

II

Whirlwind testimony
Let me confess to nothing about my father, you should know his
type
I'll have to climb the family tree to find where the madness
started

<Runs in the blood>

His love for murder taught me how to look for outer space in the
eyes of a corpse
It's not madness if this is your level of normal
Your variation of an ethic
Your adorable coda
There's a story behind every murder, a sexual conquest
Ted Bundy was a nice-looking man
I didn't know how much I enjoyed raping little girls until I
joined the army
More fun than a night at the movies

III

Daddy's monster saw me
teeth eating each other

IV

I shuddered upon the threshold
entryway, my first home away
bruised eyes camouflaged by night
sarcophagi yawned
found her on the desert planet
cold flower with scant bloom
this is a new burning for her
I have no plan for the pieces

V

Four years gone
my father's murder trial
bones in the basement,
treasure trove sacked
When I came home from the service he
was in an institution
When I came home from the service he
was strolling across perfectly-manicured
lawns
When I came home from the service he
smiled, often, traipsing the green

This is good behavior
He remembered all the pretty faces
and mine

VI

We spoke of Thanksgiving and dipping eyes
into Ranch dressing, skull cup
the vessel is not screaming
tentacles drip from
(and we gave thanks)

VII

Convalescent miracle sunglow
"Parlor tricks and a deck of cards on fire"
he said, when I sat beside him
"Their names are adorable, but make sure
each one is different, no two Jessicas"
I just want to fuck my sister when he's talking
      noir prisons glance at this morning
       —his good behavior rewarded with light
"I'm on the cover of a magazine"
names in the heat sound like sleeping mysteries
their eyelashes beneath my fingernails
explosions aged their souls but not their flesh
"How many sand snakes did you fill with your come?"
Angels devouring-crunching on breastplates
      picking their teeth with vaginal
      sluice in jaw-collapse

VIII

I had to make sure I was ready to see my sister. I heard she was married, in letters and phrases, broken things settling to the bottom of my stomach… "He will do as we require" alleyways find me the runaways, with my gun, there is… "My business isn't with you, son, you can run or you can die" let us watch him sacrifice heroism as his feet piston the concrete, nearly tripping on garbage as he flees into nothing, and the girl looks up with my gun pointed against her forehead, cold steel and big wet eyes, she is only sixteen at the most and I cannot describe her features and you'll know why in a moment, "Swallow the whole thing or you die" she did as she was told until vomit erupted volcanic, her jaw doing such a sweet job until I throbbed and rushed and jettisoned, this brave little one who ran away from everything until to find it here waiting for her, well, you know, she could have tried to bit me but she wanted to live and it was interesting how much brain was in her head when it exploded against the concrete wall, and I think she knew I was going to do it because as I came her eyes didn't widen but they narrowed and looked into my eyes, diamonds of blood painting the graffiti, waterfalls of brick, meat inside of an open face, semen found its way to her brain "He will do as we require." There might be stars somewhere.

IX

Rooms filled with yellow light are with me
Interiors of home, I have seen father

and sister climbed my shoulders and ripped
at me,

we have a man who will take the fall
(I dreamed we had a mother once)
hands pull us down into the carpet
I said her name

pumped her full of my name
(and I also ate worms from
open Iraqi stomachs
like mouths
and I ate them
and I said,
and I said
a name that might have been my mother's
and I also
chewed the wet worms
for the sake of avarice
true love
prayer
country

Walter can hear us
Margaret does not see my face
she says

X

Walter has found his version of Earth below us
Your face is sculpted from mother,
medusa head of surrendered halos
wilt thou sing this moonlight of sorrow's-call

when you were a baby FATHER showed me
scriptures in your flesh
you know mother couldn't help but scream
rememberances hold us, water park bathrooms
wilt thou sing this moonlight of sorrow's—call

cutting out the obivion in all of us
this is not an apology
I left to find God in the desert with a gun
but God did not have a gun
the children slept upon landmines
arterial spray does not ask for forgiveness
wilt thou sing this moonligh of sorrow's—call

every woman I killed in the desert had your name
interior of altar-space
the sand was naked in the evening
oh yes, a metaphor for misadventures
I see the past through the grainy lens
glasses crushed in the fist of a minotaur
wilt thou sing this moonlight of sorrow's—call

fury painted the flags I couldn't find
houses full of things that were gone
I was not enraged
but I wanted to be the man of my dreams
instead I found FATHER'S face
upon the foundation of a broken bridge
fissures, scorpions, heat-lightning
wilt thou sing this moonlight of sorrow's—call

XI

Counting
my lack of artifacts

the unkept—unfound—unknown
anhiliation in the era
subjugation

Holes in the ceiling
starmap

souls burning into black
the girls I've murdered
or watched

all the same
gone without a trace

pulsation of tragic
carved spasms

there is no such thing as war
charcoal nuggets—
children without eyes

little boys
who will never ride horses

Russian tanks
bone composite

the cigarettes of bored men
neighborhoods collapse
under fire

I have laughed before

XII

Envelope cracks
alone in the house for this
OH WHERE WERE YOU

when I was abused by my FATHER
you are so concerned about
disorders
war trauma

THERAPHY IS AVAILABLE
in case I have been fucked
by blood vision
they cannot be sued

the government, the military
they want to help

HERE'S OUR HAND, OPEN
don't attack shopping malls
or schools
or campgrounds
or military installations
with machine guns
unless you have seen us

let us save you, help you
        but that is why I sought the desert
        the heat
        where blood followed me
        my sister never wrote back
        pictures of girls in wallets
        look like the ones I've eaten

listen to a broken heart crumble
blank check apocalypse

XIII

We are syndromes in sepia
cancer-soaked planetary core

subscriptions to megalopolis
cancelled plagues

abuse in the afternoon
talk shows, fortresses

a lifetime of television
disorder in the court

glory be to the praetors
books with gold pages

we have kingdoms and mirrors
expectations for the young

we devour during hurricane
season
a sister lies in bedsheets

this convent, chalices of rust
slow jazz for this month

we are free, my love
now I shall dedicate a sonnet

Entry 8

Walter and I spoke today for the first time. For clarification purposes, I should explain that Walter and I have been exhanging mild pleasantries for a time, and today I stoppped while he was watering his lawn. Pansie urinated on his bush, and that allowed me to feign embarrassment. He was clearly nervous. He coughed several times, and often looked up and down the street.

Finally, I came out with it and said, "You're looking for your parole officer."

He was awkward for several moments, but when he finally admitted to it, I could see his shoulders lose their tension. He wants to speak the truth.

"Don't worry about it," I said. "If I was worried about a child molestor attacking me in broad daylight, I wouldn't walk my dog by your house every day." I didn't let that sting him. I kept going. "I actually feel kind of bad for you. I bet you just want to move on with your life."

It felt like a door opened between us and we both stepped through. We continued to talk. We decided to go get coffee together. He believed that I was interested in him, which is important, because I am interested in him. He must feel safe with me.

I promised him I would not bring the dog. I took Pansie home and came back. In that short time, he had changed into a polo shirt, and I think he brushed his teeth. I could smell the Colgate on his breath. I was close enough to smell him. We walked together.

—Becca

WALTER
(PRIMED NUMBERS)

I

These phantoms of us
      Brick molded
She is so pure I mean
blue flame eyes caged
whipfallen lashes close
do lips remember
      unwashed shores
do lips
      pilgrims knelt
course these fingertips
      in Heaven you will not scream
Graffitti surrenders your voice
Recorded-looped-recorded
To whom these cries
Feel like shut eyes
pure phantom lifted

II

Our honeymoon involved ruins
in these spaces falling good soldiers
museum-history rotate
children ran through this
place, laughing
water balloon war
genesis of the faces

she didn't hold my hand
I see it, earth-sucked blood
murder is sacrifice to God

look how happy

       Her vengeance
silence over dinner
reign now, chins, lips

upon her chest ripped
watch the feed

those children, heirs to genesis
one cried
water slap violence

victory is murder
in a honeymoon glow

III

Mr. Vegas returned
Expectations, I know I know

his stride sleeps in the house
Now do I hear

Await the delicate design
I don't want to go outside today
Sunlight my sins

Did I kill her?
In prison I looked into eyes
(Did I kill them)
      In the dark of filth
      we are pure
      all pure
uniform impregnate forgiveness
Even there

Mr. Vegas could speak
the filth had a face
how many bodies
NUBILE, OH, OH,
"play this year's game"

IV

"I remember the first time,
boy, I tell you what! Ha,
yeah, hahahahaha, yeah! Tears,
man, running down your face."

Here I am thinking it's a gift
for such a slovenly piece,
that first time, brought her home
while he spasmed into his sister
my wife
my grave warden
now he reminds me

viagara injection, primed

"And when she arched her back
you couldn't wait, not one minute
and damn, you just kept… HAMMERING
that poor thing,
and her, only TWELVE hahahahahaha, man
what a good time.
Hymens are a funny thing
you know."

I am beyond this now. This pain does not belong here.

Breaking me down again. Return me to this prison,
from one abyss to another

"You went back for seconds! You know why?"

You were staring at me, Mr. Vegas.
You and Margaret, hands on each other's sex
and I thought I was damned
I know why
I know why

She whispered her name into my ear
I always wondered why
even now
just her name, so drugged,
maybe she saw God,
or me, and introduced herself,
while I gritted my teeth

Crystal broken everywhere.
Her favorite rainbow was college.
Just her name, bloody spread thighs.

V

Caricatures in theraphy clothes
        reminds me of ghosts frozen in glass pictures
        a no-smoking therapy session
        we all signed the paperwork

Suicidal, obssessive-complusive, lovestruck
        the veterans look at the clock
        salvation was supposed to taste like summer
        we do not speak

Some of you are here on court-order
        justice bleeds behind her dress
        bottles of approved chemical disorder
        my eyes are blinking slow today

Words spoken in compendium prose
        what vile sorcery, necromancer
        plays on a slow violin
        even the Greeks wrote about murder

On condition, your health is at stake
        my health is at stake
        fit into this map of nothing
        turn us all invisible

Appendectomy of afterbirth
        your temporary salutation
        sickness deviates, hymnal emergence
        therapy is the galaxy of obvious carnality

        Caricuratures of therapy clothes
        Suicidal, obssessive-complusive, lovestruck
        Some of you are here on court-order
        Words spoken in compendium prose
        On condition, your health is at stake
        Appendectomy of afterbirth
        Let me show you the way

VI

A crooked doll lies upon the grass
lost in the park, my haven
I know the detective watches
waiting for the leper to dream again

> the girl from the window
> breathes the same clouds

> she stops before me,
> calf display, dog urination

I know what the detective is thinking
therapy, pills, breaking the law
his glory
willing to risk the life of this girl
to play the role of a good man

> "I have seen you
> watching me."

I don't know what I am thinking
write to your wife
> *(she is not here now*
> > *we exist in parceled-absences*
> > *I should know more)*

I want the sunlight-birthed shadows to move
knuckle collapse
walls that glow in the dark of prison

> "My name is Becky,
> and you're Walter."

We are all so, all so,
all… so…

VII

She already knows the name of sex offenders
Becky and coffee in bright
window glare
Pre-apology syndrome tightens veins
throbbing doom between glances
if she can forgive,

she is fascinated with the code in my blood
now I understand
—women like her—
        girls

one of them in prison
suggested my life was a disease
not my fault
like a priest who believeth

would I have been saved by her denial
Mr. Vegas was a ghost in prison
on paper

now one day Becky can write
a paper for her class
redemption, malaise
origins of hurt
she'll make an excellent liar when she grows up

VIII

I am wondering when I will see her again
I am wondering if I have died
Breathing labored, pain,
Needles inside my chest
I want to see her again
She won't speak, she will listen
She won't exist, she isn't real
But that's okay because the idea of her

Legs—
is enough
My masters cannot
know she lives
inside of me, inside of me
they cannot know she is

inside of me, a spider dancing
on the underside of my ribcage
I must keep my love secret
she is young and they will hurt her
ask me to hurt her
on display, necrophilic eyes, necrophilic veins
they will make her wet by opening her stomach
they will spread the blood
I know how they laugh at the bread metaphor
but that is flesh
that is mind.

IX

"Where were you yesterday…" both of them chew and ask about
my redemption, because I am not supposed to be a good man,
but I am here, and I am… "We have work to do…" I don't know
what I can be… "Our father has asked about all the pretty girls
who are not screaming inside of the pit…"

Entry 14

I would like to continue with observations from my last entry. While I have found it easy to break Walter down, I find his lonesomeness very endearing. I want to be near him, hold his hand, brushing his fingertips. There is a rattle in his throat when he chokes back tears. While he tells me his story, I cannot look away from him. I cannot record my thoughts. I must listen to him.

And in the evenings, when I'm alone, I hear him. In school, I hear him. I see the things that he has done. I see the things that he has been forced to do.

I should pity myself. I was never strong enough to handle this. I thought I would approach it all with the calm of a focused researcher, but this man's tears have stopped my pen. When I am with him, I want to go home, and when I am home, I want to be with him. I dread being with him, but I am helpless. It's as if his nightmares are feeding my head.

Margaret, Mr. Vegas. Margaret, Mr. Vegas. The things their father did to them. I want to write them. I want to write down every single scream that Walter recounts. He apologizes over and over again for his trembling hands. He wants me to hold him, but he is afraid. I do not think he is afraid of himself, but rather, what Margaret and Mr. Vegas have done to him. He does not truly believe the thing they created was left to die in prison.

Last night, Walter confessed that his wife and her brother were "working" again. It was the only thing he told me at the diner. It was the only thing he brought with him, and he left me with it. Alone.

—Becca

DETECTIVE
(JOURNALSCOPE)

I

Another Albanian family diner
hardy har har
they know my coffee style
  Kristina
  should be with her friends

Hardworking and (can't think of another word my thoughts)

"The usual," I tell her.

She smiles.
  Before I taste
What would I think?
   (know thy enemy
   they teach you to know them
   be them,
   to stop
   them)

Two missing blondes this month
I am your protector
Because I know my enemy
(I don't think Walter is at fault... but there
is... something... I am... learning)

I come here and see with Walter's eyes

"How're your grades?" I ask her. A nice girl.
This stoic gentleman inquires.

With a smile,
"Very good."

Of course they are.
Here's your return smile.

II

Call and visit.
How simple?

For me. I can't.
What else? Strangers with children,
broken women
internet dating

THIS MAN RAPED LITTLE GIRLS
and his name is Walter.
Their bodies were never found.
I will protect the community.

But I don't. Want to see him.
I want to know him.

From the comfort
of my own car and stink
I watch,

girl runs with dog past his house,
WALTER, DO YOU SEE HER LEGS?

I see her legs.
Kristina's legs might be.
Young.

Curtain-slip. Is it him?
Do you watch her while I watch her?
Do you watch me watch you watch her?

A girl will hurt before I catch you in the act.
You will do it again.
I promised Kristina without speaking.

That's the lottery ticket life of a detective

Okay, my shield is unclean
curtain slip

I haven't thought about my ex since Walter
walked out of that computer screen
    This marriage is simple.
    Me. The street.
    Curtains.

III

Drapery, parts
Wolf mask, brother
Me, watching
Viewing, siblings
Nude, together
Walter, downstairs
Deserve, This
Oh, no
Brother, inserts
Window, open
Wolf mask, plastic
brother-sister
I want to tell

somebody
a mouthful of sand now

IV

"The coffee is delightful, as always,
Kristina."

A boy her age should be on his knees
"Princess, let me give you galaxies."

Walter smelled blood

Did his wife—willingly?
My wife—ex-wife…?

I shudder to
no
I won't know

"Kristina, your smile always brightens
my day."

Did Walter stick his hands inside
a Kristina-type?

Last night, the brother's penis
Throbbing, Quivering
Blood-slick

"I think a cheeseburger will be good.
Early lunch and all."

What an interesting life you've had
(the FATHER)
wicked sanitarium picture
oh what I do now, what I do
the files I don't have

no wonder
deleted, deleted, deleted
classified

who is this patriarch bleeding like

where he once lived
hehehehehehehe, such a good worker
excellent with a mop and bleach

no smoking sir, but that voice, they say,
raspy

okay now
in this silence I wonder
who you are

how much they have given me
not even a beat cop
insanity is out of my league
so are sanitariums

and old fathers

the man who put Walter
into a block
he met this man I see

my league of nations
all kinds of cities
and faces like these

well, shit, I'm a free man
hunting free men

II

I spoke to you in your chair, a tired man

retired, what did you retire

"this man, Walter, you remember"
your eyes merged
memories rearranged and I waited

"just his parole officer," you said
what I would give now to have seen
your house was empty
spent, exhausted, a man in a chair
I do not look for mirrors
your advice involved a vain disappearing act

"parole officer
forget it
look at me
forget it
go back
he's just a man"
hell licks my lips
this taste of malaise

"the father
you already know
met him
robbing a bank
shot a man's face
saw the brain
on the wall
licked it

wiped it
smeared it
on his face
insanity plea worked"

I left you lying in your chair
I left you with those nightmares
and an empty house
a palace without a realm
vanishing among blank lawns
quiet houses
there are no dogs on this street

VI

I know that I am partaking in an investigation
Please don't let this be an investigation
It is not my intention to partake in an investigation
swallow pills and sunlight and that's it, that's all
this is not an investigation
I don't know what anyone is doing here
There is something I will find

      INSERT THE TWIST

here
     is
         the
             twist
                  find
                      me
descend
descend

why do fathers get involved
this is not an investigation
I promise myself, promised myself
when will I speak to my ex-wife for the last time
(LET ME SPEAK THE WORDS NOW, LET ME REMEMBER
THEM FOR ALL TIME, LET ME THINK ON IT, LET
ME THINK ON IT, DREAMS, HICCUPS, DREAMS,
CATACLYSMS IN REVERSE, divorce
divorce
diverse

I never wanted it, it was you, I never wanted it)

This is not my fault
This is all my fault
It is not an investigation

Now I chase a killer, a ghost, a paragon, a mortal monster
why don't I

call you, let you know I'm okay
YOU SAID I COULD
why this moment now, why this moment now

I cannot feel these fingers
        everything trembles on somebody else's edge
let me call you

I'm okay, I'm okay
this is not an investigation
I am not out of my league

don't think about the Albanian girl
she is too young
there are crimes within crimes within crimes
crimes don't exist until they are committed
I have not committed a crime

I
NEVER
WANTED
THIS

if you lingered in Heaven and looked at me now
come back in time spirit, come back in time
visit this real
spit on me with thunderstorms
just not
silence

I have felt that silence
"just going out with the fellas"
IT WAS JUST A FEW BEERS
I said, I said

This is not an investigation
Feel my pulse and
let me breathe

call you, call you

TILL DEATH

do us part, we part
apart
so many variations of murder

I hurt inside and I was afraid to hurt
this is me now
not an investigation
this is me
God, if I believed
I'm going to talk to a man
who ate brains
who influenced rape
maybe killed others

I am not a detective
JUST SIT, AND WATCH
PERCEIVE
don't let him talk to young girls

VII

Brickwork under day
Electric hum parking lot
Tremors in waiting
Concrete whispers blackened dread
Napoleonic dead zone

VIII

"Have you got enough bleach…" the secretary is bored, her eyes
do not move… "Is this an official investigation…" I am a visitor,
from this planet I arrive "You will find him in his chair…"
sanitariums in Florida might have lizards on the walls, or in
the walls, inside of mass-confusion prophecies "He is always
alone, that man…" so pleasant to be around, maybe even in a
graveyard "There is patience inside of the television at night…"
someone speaks.

IX

Looking for the concept of windows
wet earth,
move aside for jawbones
dust-rattling memories of fog

Kristina
her being here was something else
when I dropped her over my shoulder
among the dead trees
ash trees, weather cracked
broken bones
evening sleeps for miles across the highway
let them find her in a creak
let the dogs put their noses into
the dirt

a dark overture to dance beneath
how like an object this flesh resists
pile of woman in the uncivilized world
I'm supposed to walk away

or leave a mark because I want to
be found by murder-drunk detectives
and perpetual jackets in journalism throes

***

truth is, having violent sex is fun
the rush of power dwells here among brittle leaves
the next girl might be prettier, virginal

I think she'll never regret
mistakes she cannot make now
no need to gloat or mutilate
you never forget your fist Victim

how is she a victim?

her name will be forgotten or it will
simply be a name that has ended
a conclusion rather than a story with
an ending, as if nobody wrote about
her or birthed her
she is not a victim
but an expression

***

Professors dissect historical moments
and literature
and poems
and philosophy
to invent new context
let's learn about megalomania so we never see it again
they will analyze me and wonder what I looked like and why I
killed
the girl
because if they know me

—they can stop me—
the next time or at least
stop more of me

***

My name might be the subject
of a novel or court case
I'll enter the pages
of a killer compendium
and I get more than fifteen minutes of fame
because I am not you
or them
or anyone else
this is my expression and of course
there's a disease that goes along with it
something already named

***

Look at her

we have junkyards
and graveyards
she would be just as silent and forgotten
in a junkyard
like a toy
a child has outgrown

***

There's nothing poetic about a dead woman
who was raped
murdered
and dropped into the woods

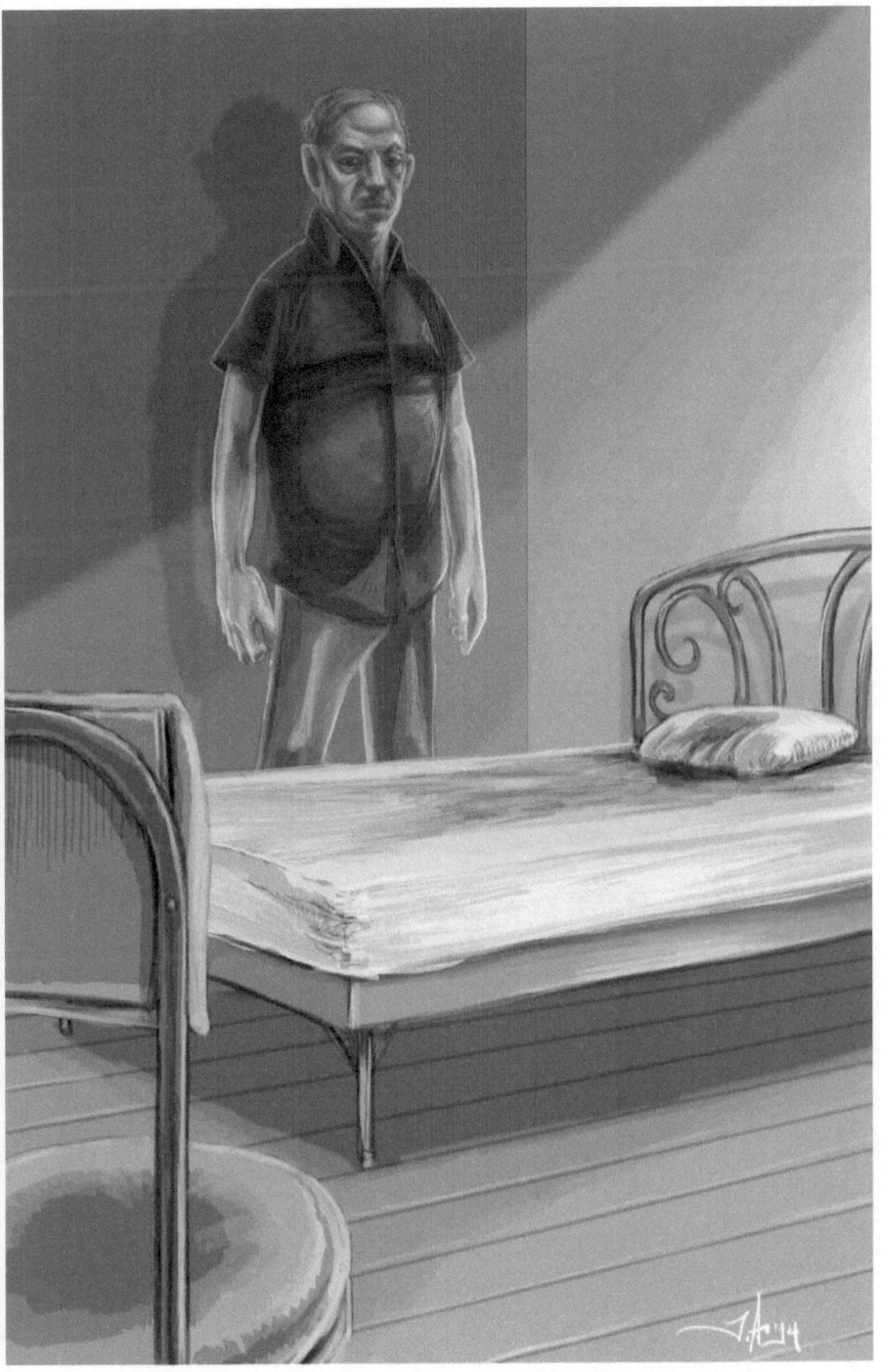

X

What he told me
what he said
what I remember
what he did
what he looked like
what he said
what he remembered
what I know
what he didn't say
what he left behind
what his parents knew
what his blood knows
what his children do
what his voice sounds like

there was was sunlight in the room
there was darkness in the room
there was a man in the room
there was a discussion in the room
there was a bed in the room
there was a man in the room
there was a chair in the room
there was a killer in the room

destinies, nightmares, soundeffects
basements, holes, slabs
concrete, masks, there are no masks
corpses, water parks, parking lots

I am no longer here
I am no longer there
I am no longer visible
I am no longer spared
I am no longer innocent

I am no longer alive
I am no longer this man
I am no longer
I am no
I am
I

Entry 15

*Two weeks have passed since my last entry. I have not seen
Walter. I have not walked past his house. I have been home sick
from school most of the time, or late. I do not want to go. I have
not had the desire to write, or to do much at all. I know that my
"illness" is a sort of "depression." I think it's more than that,
but isn't it always? I mean, isn't depression just a simple word
for a sense of damnation that is unique to one person alone, a
sense that nobody else can possibly understand?*

*Certainly, they will empathize. They will encourage me. They
will tell me to change my routine. Exercise. Join a club. Or gang.
They will give me a slip of paper with medications scribbled on
it, and I will be cured. I will be motivated. I will walk among the
living again.*

*Walter talked about this once. He talked about his reliance on
the medications, and how he hates himself for it. But he wants to
be a better man. He wants to be the man he wanted to be when
he met Margaret, before they married, before she showed him
the pit underneath her father's house.*

*Isn't all of this so predictable? My obsession has become
another cliché archetype. Watch me use big words to describe
my malaise.*

*Someone has to know. Someone has to have seen that pit, but
nobody has done a fucking thing about it. There isn't anything
there but the echo of long-forgotten screams, screams that don't
belong to faces anymore. That's what Walter said. That's how he
described it. And I keep thinking that.*

*I was supposed to be a researcher. I was supposed to crack this
case, understand who Walter is, reveal the power behind his
deeds. I was going to bring justice to the dead souls of dead
girls people have forgotten about. Some of them probably never
made headlines. Walter said that, too. He said it used to bother*

Mr. Vegas when nobody cared. Margaret and their father had planned everything carefully, too carefully. Nobody was supposed to know. There were not supposed to be headlines, but Mr. Vegas wanted them.

And they are "working" again.

Now, I am an accomplice. I know that Mr. Vegas wants to be caught, and so does Margaret. And yet, nobody can connect the dots. Nobody has opened any kind of formal investigation into the family. Why?

I have seen Walter's parole officer outside of my house. But why? I don't know. I can only guess, and I don't want to. I don't want this anymore. Nobody is strong enough for this. Nobody is strong enough to handle Walter's damnation.

I am trapped here. I am trapped in these words and I am trapped in all this bullshit. I have ripped pages out and burned them. Why not burn the whole thing?

I can't do it. I'm not strong enough. But if I did, I could move on, couldn't it? Wouldn't it be cathartic?

I'm a senior. I'm going to graduate soon. I will be an adult. I will be responsible for my own life.

And I often wonder: Does Walter like me? Is he attracted to me? Am I too old for him? Why doesn't he want to kill me?

Why doesn't he try to kill me?

And these thoughts are insane. I hate myself for wondering these things. I hate myself more and more every day for everything that I have done, and for thinking I could just hop-skip-jump my way into a child molestor's life and think that maybe I could SAVE THIS MAN. Maybe I could HELP HIM FIND REDEMPTION even though they fucking said HE IS HEALED, HE IS NOW A FREE MAN.

How pathetic. I just needed to write. I needed a wall to scream at. But this isn't everything. This isn't all of it. I want to translate my venom into Chinese and Portuguese. I want to people that their children will never be safe, can never be safe, because

*there will always be Margaret and Mr. Vegas and Walter. The
father will always live. He's in an institution now, and I should
visit him. I should speak with him. I should know his mind.*

But I do know his mind. I am inside of his mind, right now.

*There is only one way
to end this
for me
I must have him
come here
my parents are not
home
they are never home
this weekend
in my house
the condemned man*

—B

MARGARET
(PSYCHO-CYS)

I

Let's see how babies born of rape
are aborted
hahaha
You think my woman's body
with father in the room
put her on the stairs and watch

blood rivers the stairwell
fifteen and a whore
allow this education
so nice to let my brother go first
Walter stand by Father and observe

he came all this way
my brother came inside her again
miscarriage in the afternoon with coffee in the kitchen
Walter do you think you would have had a son

but that's okay, my womb
has been a fair playground
I know what she felt like

but she was a coward.

II

Married and wounded the hart
OH YOU WERE TALKING TO ME, FATHER
thy commandments
thou shalt not watch horror films
FOR
thanksgiving we shall eat the eyes
what Heavens have delighted
vitreous stuffed the stomach lining
the three of us held hands
THANK YOU FATHER
and he said nothing
his affair with god
head bowed as he sat like a rubber baron
in his throne of wood

III

>Can you hear me
I could hear him
>Have you visited Father
I have not decided to answer
the convalescent
I never wanted his blood on my brain
>You should be responsible

> *you disappeared*
> *left me with Father's desire*
> *he showed me what I need of you*
> *I opened*
> *he closed*
> *I married*
> *he went insane*
> *you came back*
> *Walter took the fall*
> *don't you know*
> *he is a godly man and won't admit it*
> *he is stuffed with redemption*

>Walter is staring out the window
he is trapped in someone else's nightmare
>The cop came by again yesterday
Father told you to never be afraid
>Walter has been away. I don't know where he is going
this is us, you, our destiny
>Do you still want to...?
the last baby, I wanted to keep
and didn't tell you
no
the last three
>I want you on your hands and knees
of course
what I want

>You should have seen the fire-dripped sky, the limbs that
blasted into the air
men stepped on IEDs.
I have seen the fire-dripped sky
>I hope you are bleeding today, like you said you would be
Walter is going to break us
brother
he is going to break us
I am no longer your sister, lover, concubine
the limbs that blasted into my air
prisons taste like metal

IV

I always wonder if he wants an apology
while he pretends to sleep through life
in his bed now, twilight
so he won't hear me screaming
my life is the terminal Auschwitz

Walter
it's me

I know

You are seeing a girl, a young girl

(his eyes find me in the dark)

ask her to kill us
Walter, it is the last thing
the only thing
you see, we are not here
our universe is beneath our feet
all the things we've taught you
your sentence is self-imposed
Mr. Vegas will not find you
my body does not belong to me
murder, I don't recall murder
I see days and things that were done as a matter of course
how many children thrown into the abyss
wailing
because we must cull them
we must not deny who we are
but I made you
and you are breaking these chains
please

you want me to ask someone
to kill you

us

hahahahahahahahaha
you
are asking
hahahahahhahahaha

you think we should be rehabilitated
healed
let the system code our souls
give us God or homosexual gang rape
(Walter's delicate answer
is not here

in rendered shadow concepts)

V

versions of cathartic fingers trace
look upon us
      I have set these planets in motion

"officer, I want to make a confession"

that is all I had to say,
      and here he sits

"…even my grandfather…"
a puppet's head bounces

"… I like the way their mouths open when they know…"
      "our father is not insane, but enlightened"
      "you know my mother's murder was unsolved"
      "I just want to be caught"
I wonder why I cannot be a human being, when I see so many
others weep upon the vision-threat of genocide, because I don't
feel like I belong to this species, yet here I am, even though I think
about it often, not counseling or cognitive therapy of any kind, but
rather complete termination. I wonder why I cannot be a human
being because everything I think a human is I am not, but I am a
stranger or a monster or something unlike both those things and
altogether different like a clock without a shadow. If you gave
me the proper medication or removed hemispheres of brain what
would you learn about me that would ultimately mean something,
anything, to anybody. I can give you the story. You can write a
book about the girls I've helped murder, and you can be the hero,
you can sit at the trial, and you will be at the premiere when a
famous actor depicts your face in a film version of this horror.

but it is not horror
"are you afraid, officer?"

he is not sure
this conversation may not be happening
and that is okay

VI

a hammer and nails
aisle 6
lye
bleach
409
windex
rubber gloves
latex gloves
a mop
a mop bucket
batteries
a flashlight
pliers
monkey wrench
wire coat hangars
this place has everything
which aisle can I find…
this one, ma'am
all these instruments
all the convenience
one stop shopping
a diet coke for the road
of course the cashier is smart and won't put it in the bag
beep
beep
beep
that'll be…
the value of someone's life
you really can place a dollar amount
no, I'll take the coke with me, thank you
the cashier has a smile full of teeth
she is maybe
seventeen

god geez it looks like I'm going to kill someone with all
this stuff
hahahaha
yeah
have a good day, ma'am
thanks, you too

VII

(the woman walked the stairs
        she imagined skulls beneath her feet
        but there was a time
        yes, there was
        when she left school early
        half day
        elementary school
        Mom always picked her up
        but Mom wasn't there
        not this time
        Margery ran into the park
        found her mom on the swing
        a smile on her face
        "swing with me," she said
        that was a time
        oh yes that was a time
        "I got all of them right on my math test!"
        Mom laughed
        because Margery was so pleased with herself
        birds probably flew overhead
        clouds would have moved slowly
        but those clouds might not have been there
        trees
        the park had tress
        or did it?
        and we cannot know
        if Mom really could play the violin
        like she did in the pictures
        but there was no music in those pictures
        only the image of music
  as the woman walked up the stairs)

Entry 16

Oh, Walter, if you read this
I am sorry
I don't know why I feel the need to apologize I just... can't finish
my thought
you tasted like sunshine and earth
I thought about God and
all those girls you killed who didn't have fathers
I know you'll never
read this
my thoughts... I don't know... I don't know... help me....
so much for justice
there is no justice
theire is no justice
only fucking and hate and blood and fists and violence and
fucking, everything is about fucking and everything revolves
around fucking, our entire species and I am just another
wretched animal trying to survive and I am just like every
organism every damn thing I am not anything special I want to
fuck and be fucked and I want to own and be owned and I want
to look into the pit and think about what is down there and a part
of me wonders what it is like to be down there where it is dark
and there is nothing
there is nothing

WALTER
(OUR BOLD CONFEDERACY)

I

I never wanted

     believe

I never

Let me start over
This is what you want and I will give you anything I can
I shouted at prison walls
and now you want me to say these things
make them real
give the ghosts life
when I have always been too goddamned weak

   in prison they
   oh god
   they
made me see it when I didn't want to
DON'T YOU KNOW WE'RE ALL INNOCENT AND WE'RE
ALL GUILTY
I think that was the motto etched upon a brick wall
somewhere between a grassland and a basketball net and a pack
of cigarettes
spray paint
fences
let me tell you a story
I fell in love with a woman named Margaret
and there was a chair
I don't remember the worlds I visited
but in the chair I urinated
starlight dust upon my lips
   Becca, please
   as much as I'd like to come in your mouth
   I prefer to be a saint now
PLEASE
don't take me back there

you've a library of serial killer books
everything is HELTER-SKELTER
but I am not a god
you are my friend
poor girl
my friend
you're the addiction and the cure
the test and the trial
those curls
do you know I never

                                                                  wanted
                                                                  to be

I raped and murdered nine girls
all of them under the age of sixteen
but they let me sit next to you
I'm on parole

II

Nothing will unite an empire faster
than sports
Mr. Vegas and his sister placed a bet
spinning
      the confluence
spinning
and we have digest language in plaster-phases
Margaret laughed and said

"but virgins have been sacrificed to stop rain"

there are no apologies
while we exorcise these walls
pyramids for gods and dead flesh
altars for women who will no longer breathe
why do you want to know if I am here
monsters drag saints to Hell
mary was a virgin
raped by
it was not a crime
intervention
three kings crossed the desert
but walter, this confirms

messiahs are born from rape
hardship
divorce
poverty
anxiety

depression
malnutrition

there is no such thing as crime
if you can find Heaven in black spaces

III

the officer and I stood on my porch
we talked about Becca, how beautiful she is
how damaged
he nodded his head
silence
shadows beneath his eyes
comforting his lips
this generation is supposed to know my name
according to his thoughts
he doesn't come by as often
preferring the silence of his own damnation
"you've survived a long time out here in the wilderness"
I don't have an answer
he isn't looking into my eyes
a Tom Cruise film is on television
involves aliens and guns
he comes into the house with me
"where is your wife, her brother?"
I can't remember

IV

Beers crack and weeds
outside swelter

The detective wants to talk. He feels awkward. I have
invited him into my home. I have molested and raped girls.
Young girls. And now he knows that I have a young friend.
What does he want to talk about? He is a melancholy man,
a stereotypical, noir-detective with nothing better to do than
crusade. I understand that he wants to be a good man. I also want
to be a good man.

"I've been trying to figure out why a teenage girl would
want to be your friend," he said.

"I've been trying to figure out why you're harassing
me," I said.

He sipped his beer. "You're such a nice guy," he said.

"I don't appreciate sarcasm. I don't think this is funny."

"What's supposed to be funny?" he asked.

We both sat there for a long time.

"You're so timid," he said. "You can barely work up the
nerve to talk to anybody. Can't even make eye contact with me.
You don't look at your wife. I've seen what she does. With her
brother. Your brother in law."

What else does he know? There is much I can tell him.

"Their father is locked up in an asylum. But you knew
that."

He is trying to understand something I cannot teach
him. He is trying to learn something important instead of just
watching me. I have violated my parole. But he isn't here to tell
me this. He isn't here to arrest me. To warn me.

Let him stare at the beer can.

"They let you go because you're a different man now."

They let me go because I'm a different man now. I sat in
front of the parole board and talked about God. I don't believe in

God. But I did not want to hurt that girl. I didn't want to hurt any girls. Ever.

"You had good parents," he said. "No history of mental illnesses."

No history of mental illnesses.

"What is it?" he asked.

"I don't understand."

He nodded his head. "Maybe I do. Maybe I understand that you're helpless. If you're helpless, you can tell me. Tell me now and we can save that girl's life. Together."

Nobody will hurt Becca.

"She isn't in danger," I said.

I could tell him many things about murderers, about archaic traditions,

bloodlines

V

I thought of legs many times in prison
      the dog licks his teeth at me
and here this bleed

just the first girl, the first time
or one that you remember
      but
      you see
      I don't remember how many
      I impregnated
I am not afraid of truth
oh yes,
tell me about truth
      the dog's face has disappeared
      don't you see

who is talking to whom
      let the investigation puzzle over me
      engimas sleep
      in your words
her vagina tasted like cinnamon
hanging from a shower curtain
pinned to a nightmare
      everything becomes words
      that is the story unwritten
there are no words
no barriers to my pain
      I would hold you
I would hold you
      there are two
      of us here
how shall I taste
      when the dog
      looks again

          beady eyes
nothing to see here
they said that, you know
          nothing to see
length of time uprising
the tip of misdirection

VI

I dreamt of a glass pit
but I did not have
legs
swimming, windmill
arms

> misdirection
> midsection
> vivisection
> the meat is… so… um… she said… wet, at first

Becca couldn't speak with her mouth full
at the table

VII

he stands outside of my room
I am collected here
shirtless,
we are both
WAIT I JUST
there is no place other than us

come into the basement
it smells like a tomb

you will not hurt Becca
phantoms linger in my

space

the detective said I am
timid

Margaret's face is not on

discovered
bathroom
shopping
mall
disappeared
brunette
missing

Your wife has good taste in fashion
peeling breasts from her pockets
look how underdeveloped
                        i
        think
                of
countries in a womb
amniotic massacre of species

she would have birthed
more people

spiders were inside her bladder
or now
at least they crawl

ohdon'tthinkofusascannibalswearenotcannibalsiswearit
godidon'tbelieveinyoubelieveinme

VIII

HANK WILLIAMS HAS A SPECIAL PLACE AT THIS FEAST
MY MOTHER WAS A BIG FAN
AREN'T WE ALL
AND THIS IS HOW YOU TREAT US
DENOUNCED IN LARGE PHILOSOPHIES
OH HOW PRETTY EVERYONE CAN DANCE
TOMATO SOUP IS THE CANDY DISH
THEY WON'T FIND THE GIRL
WE PROMISE
YOUR TURN NEXT TIME
COOK THE DINNER
OUR FATHER WANTS TO LOVE YOU AGAIN
WILL YOU FILM THIS GLORY
YOUR WIFE HAS THE MOUTH OF A SAINT
AND SHE WILL NOW SPEAK OF OTHER WORLDS

IX

There is cigarette smell
lingering, of yesterday
the profile of a young woman
the profile of a wandering mind

Nightmare conservatory space
her lips repeat, fingers trace
words of mind,
we talk of gods that did not appear
gods that did not answer prayers

these tragedies fail to exist
broken factories beneath cracked billboards
yellow sky, yellow sky
rooftops commandeer fledgling spirits

the silence of families
paradise profiteers over weeded planes
we dig our own caves, carved into
pavement, where imbelicic sewage
treats discarded elements

this woman gapes at social suicide
with closed eyes I envision
caves
basements
stones
brickwork over concrete
cracked floors
cracked basement floors
one light swinging, swinging
one light swinging over the floor
the cracked concrete floor

questions of blood
"Take this cup"

take this cup away from me

confessions splattered iron walls
I have been here before
unlight, butterflies that cannot dream
sweat upon evening silence concepts
profile of a woman

incomplete dreams
lawnmowers at work
I often looked upon the broken concrete
I didn't look into their eyes

most confessions have disappeared
behind the veil of stars
a hidden veil, an invisible veil
I have nothing more to share

I don't want to disappoint you
the profile of a young woman
I was saved by the dark of concrete
brick, loneliness, squealing iron hallways
there are no wounds beyond the walls
Mr. Vegas will require me
but now there are two versions
there are two confessions

(look up
now, from
pen and lines,
I don't mean
to frighten you
sanctimonious, renditions   spaces   worlds
)

Duality is perfection
I have not lied
your skin cannot save
I have not lied

Come to me in the desert
where the bricks have names

a pasage into the rose horizon

Come to me in the desert
we shall sing to oblivion
dance circles around obfuscated
fires
oceans

The profile of a woman
I saw myself and myself
looking into me, walls
my good behavior
inside the confessional, rot
the stench of forgotten priests

Your have studied my plague
the good-behavior man will sleep

Cannibals and snake charmers
roam the brick-floored desert
we are landscapes stuffed into confessionals
cannibals masturbating snakes

you think me grotesque
I don't remember the victims
because I wasn't there
this man was

Entry 17

I walked into the clinic and asked to speak to the man who gave birth to Margaret and Mr. Vegas. The secretary was speaking with a janitor about bleach. I kept thinking about Walter's weddding day. I thought about bright lights and stardust. I thought about uncomfortable shoes that slipped along the floor of union-owned hall.

The secretary didn't ask too many questions. She mentioned that there had been a visitor here recently, and I described Walter's parole officer. She confirmed it. Nice lady. I told her the officer was my uncle. She crinkled up her face when I mentioned it. I looked at him, but I did not see his face. He told me what my insides looked like. He told me what I might taste like. He told me a history of murder. I did not see his face.

MR. VEGAS
(I AM YOUR SAINT FOR TODAY)

I

vessels call upon languages spoken in violence
She is so beautiful, to me
which dead gods are watching through black windows
The procedure was sloppy
outside the window, a breeze touches greenery, moves

Her parents will be home soon
acceleration of blood into the drain, concentric
I want to listen to Aerosmith this time
masks fortune of littered saints upon temple
I am comfortable with our apprehension
departure into ruined convents

Father will be here, as above, so below
animals designed by a blacksmith with a bad sense of humor
The female anatomy has been a wonderful plaything
villainy is a matter of perspective
This is not goodbye

II

We must recognize moments of dire surrender
forgetting all those delicately careful morning murders
even though we are not working as negotiator's
on Hell's behalf,
Heaven's light blast,
moon glow during Passover fast,
this preaching to a family without class
staring at shards of broken glass
with millions of scorpions in the trash

We must recognize moments of dire surrender
even when we're careful how we bend her
because we're not breaking bones but touching her tender
like wrinkled old lovers
sending letters to children during frigid Decembers
lost somewhere in piles of undelivered letters
don't forget these girls were all once bedwetters

We must recognize moments of dire surrender
tonight is the last time we sit here and eat a peaceful dinner
because I wanted to die with all the war deserters
while I listened to our old man's gospel in desperate shudders
let's listen to this classic blues record performed by dead—
ah, ha, hahahahahahahahaha,
you think me acute now,
this is not some version of genius

My sister, my brother-in-law.
Ha. Ha. ha. h.
And that is the show.
Dance with me, tired skeletons.
Dance with me, foregone conclusions.
I've seen burned babies sitting in piles
of burned babies

and I have seen
before the desert, before I went,
OH MARGARET, we are
transgressions, we are
(the food
is
growing cold
fuck this
nightmare touches fingertips
nothing is as cold as it seems)

III

This is the vomit of bitterness.
And I am not a bitter man.
I have been a poem without a title.

Morning brings the promise of blood.
Through my veins, through the gutters.
Washing into the gutters.
I am not a bitter man.

Machine guns inside of suitcases.
That's what we are.
I am an explorer.
I learned these things.

Let the common headache pass.
The last shall be last.
In my sleep I have been the hanged man.
Coiling smoke, black serpents.

City washed in sand.
City washed in dead girls.

I found the dead girls in the desert.
I wanted to learn about my soul.
I learned nothing.
I know something about prisons.

IV

Everything is so right all right yes, so right all yes, okay yes, all
right, so everything
This is not the time to stop breathing the breathing to time this
stop the not
My dead fictional gods she is perfect

There is no heavy breathing. I must stop. She is not breathing.
Her eyes.
Walter you shall become a saint in someone's universe when
they write a book.
This one must have a name

The last name
Hold on, I like this song. "Big Time"… so much larger than life,
Peter Gabriel
You can be named after an angel too

No fear
She isn't afraid I think she isn't think she isn't afraid I think she
isn't
I will dance for you unravel you unnerve you

So much larger than life
This passion moves me your mouth moves me this moves the
passion your moves
You will be an immortal in the history of murder, which is the
only history, the only.

Entry 18

I am sitting here on my porch with Pansie. It's a beautiful day. The sun is about to set. I can feel the breeze. I feel calm, peaceful. I don't know why, but I'm going to Walter's. There's no reason for me to go. There is nothing there for me. I feel drawn. I feel like he wants me to be there.

I am going to walk into the house. I am going to see Mr. Vegas. I am going to see Margaret.

I am going to call the police and tell them I have been abducted. I am afraid. I am inside of the house of a man who has hurt girls before.

I will place this in my mailbox. I won't apologize for the way I feel, or the way I don't feel. The way I feel nothing. The way I feel the breeze.

Pansie has been a good dog.

—Rebecca Fuller

MARGARET
(SORCERER, HOW ART THOU BLESSED?)

I

There are no revelations from

where I sit   no secrets   vampires of present tense
I miss my mom

everything is too late

SALVATION, a curse
there is no curse   only this anonymous dark
morality, humanity
who am I to want these things

THIS LATE   game of myselffails to repeat   vast symptoms of
silence
objects fall asleep in void-form

bathroom tile painted red
she tried to cure the world through marriage

dead woman drained into a water park solace, solace
near the furnace, in the basement, this basement,
threaten moments of discomfiture

II

Helicopter angel corrupts the outer space
Let them crush lawns underfoot
marching, armed with screens and sound
we are screams, unsound
this sensation is collective and safe
newspaper vainglory, paintings, photographs
cigarette burns
morning coffee
tomorrow's helicopter angel descends for
now

III

When my brother was in the military, I went into the big
city alone. Once. I went alone and I'm not sure why. When I
went into the city, I believed I knew why I was going. I was sure
I had a purpose. I don't think that's true. I don't think I knew
what I was doing, but I did in fact go into the big city. I went
there alone.

There wasn't a particular destination that attracted my
attention. I wandered through the city and pretended not to be a
tourist. Even if you live only a few miles outside of the big city,
you might still feel like a tourist, as I did. Everyone in the city
seemed to be a stranger and a relative at the same time, and I
don't know how that's possible. I knew them and they knew me,
but I didn't know them, and they didn't know me.

Beneath my long gray jacket I wore a blue dress. A
provocative blue dress, a dress I had purchased before my
brother left me, before he gave me time to realize who I was and
what I was. I bought the dress because I hoped he would have
sex with me while I wore it. When my brother left me, I thought
I would wear it for Father, but instead, I went into the city. It was
my first time wearing the dress. It wasn't much of a dress. I had
spent so much of my time objectifying young girls, and there
was something I wanted for myself, some fantasy.

Forgive my immaturity. I wasn't married yet.

I couldn't help but feel that my family had saved some
of these girls from some inevitable horror. The girls walking
the streets. I'm not talking about the prostitutes or the wayward
girls, but the girls who lingered in retail stores and stared at
nothing. They stared slowly. Their eyes didn't move sometimes.
I watched many different girls from outside many different
establishments, and I found all their expressions were the same.
Even the workers. The working girls inside those establishments
sighed and tilted their heads and checked to see if they had
received personal phone calls. I walked inside several of the

businesses and listened to the girls talk to each other, spreading lies and speculations and worries as if they could inflict other girls with their malaise.

As the evening wore on, businesses closed. All the girls disappeared at once, as if they had been abducted or had never existed at all. The only girls left were those standing purposefully along the boulevard in provocative clothing. They were bruised women, damaged women. They never lingered for a long time. Men approached them and they disappeared into nearby structures. They disappeared into buildings.

I did not walk quickly because I thought I would attract attention to myself, but the women and the men who lingered on the boulevard seemed to know I did not belong. They seemed to know I was an invader and would not look at me more than once. They would turn their backs to me and talk to their friends in hushed tones. I could not hear them. Men eyed me but their gazes were always intercepted by a rush of bodies that closed in, bodies and voices.

The girls had becomea a display of mannequin legs. Long, plastic mannequin legs. Bare, bruised. Thick thighs locked in the fabric of flesh-clinging skirts. Father had once hung several sets of blood-dry legs from the ceiling in the chamber below our house.

I found an adult movie theater and purchased a ticket. Familiar territory for my subsconsious, a presentation of dim light ematating from somewhere. I don't know where the dim light was coming from. The movie theater's façade lorded over pavement with ancient cigarettes forever stamped into the concrete; chewing gum and discordant stains—there could have been several murders here and nobody would have reported them.

Silence. Patiently waiting city inhaled. Held its breath. crackle of screen, images, flesh
hidden beneath my jacket, a blue dress for my brother, or Father
nobody would play with me
shapes in seats
shapes and seats
this film has been watched before
practice, education

184

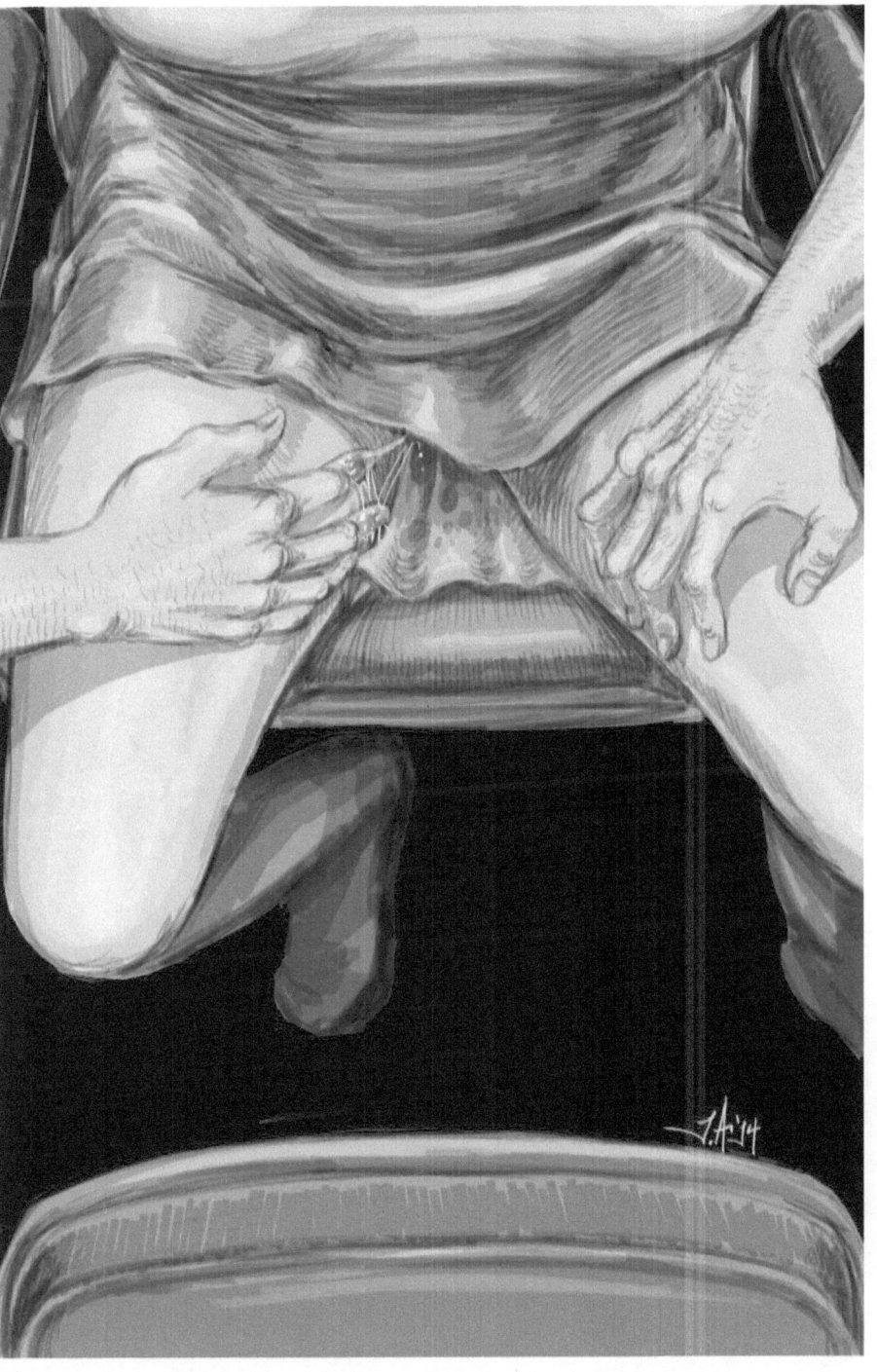

Father's rough hand inside
brother's rough hand inside
wet glass, open doorway
boys and girls playing together
my hands were always filled
dirt beneath my brother's fingernails
but that's okay
yes, that's okay
I remembered in the theater
I brought my brother
and Father, with me
my theater was always wet
inside of me and out
inner-thigh vibrato
a night at the movies
I can't remember how many men
maybe nine, or twelve
perhaps a woman among them
someone young, too
the dress was for them, in the end
the blue dress was for them
I could not wear it home
because it had been torn, lost
one man gave me a ride home
more than three times that night
Father waited up for me
tucked me in
I promised I would keep his abyss
marriage, bloodline termination
ligaments over his shoulders
Father took me home
the moon forgot me
the city, the city.

IV

uncut
lawn, bushes
visitation
detective, girl
questions
revelations, family
Father
emerges, cackles
subspecies

—humanity dreads the process of elimination
in earth-toned depths beneath streets, worlds—

captivation
reuniondesertofmisplacedformswherenothingshinesofnothing,
windows
airpsace
clouds, fields
flowers
thresholds, wind
Father

—magnificence of skull-pry
agony of remembered nightmares—

V

Within the burning river chime the clocks
Seasons wept for reaper visitations
Summer girls, autumn, fall, wintry eyes
Mouths open forever
I do not remember their names
Scalped and stained, traced by a tear

How long will her father shed a tear?
Parents wilting in gardens growing clocks
To walk with a child, point to animals, reveal the names
We are prepared for visitations
Their screams, I'll remember forever
Wrought-iron fences soaked in eyes

When I close my eyes
I do not envy a hellfire tear
Here in the house of forever
Where my father removed all the clocks
Now he awaits our visitations
He has not forgotten any names

My life is a graveyard without names
I have tasted teenaged eyes
Kidneys, bladders (of nightmare, visitations)
Vivisections provoke the wayward tear
Incinerated life clocks
Frozen in tomb-pose glory forever

Love is not forever
If my lips could move for names
Severed hands make for pretty clocks
(Mother, I have forgotten the color of your eyes)
Artifacts dusted by a single drop, one tear
We're always waiting for last visitations

I am not waiting for last visitations
Shove me into forever
My father cannot shed a tear
There is no history, there are no names
If only our cities had eyes
Our skulls would shatter into clocks

I do not have a tear for the forgotten, the names
Hell is forever in our eyes
Visitations; the burning river choked with clocks.

DETECTIVE
(I REMEMBER NOW...)

I

There's a lot of invisible laughter
But I can't hear anything, anyway
my wife used to say I'm deaf
"what are you, deaf?"
I suppose she asked me,
and I implied her understanding.
Well, arrangements of manilla folders
like flowers at a funeral
arrangements, arrangements of everything
and I'm comfortable with this
arrangement. I'm quite insane
for slipping into an old man's shadow.
I wanted to learn about something,
but I forgot what.
Just supposing, I might not be
changed, in a field of caskets.
I don't have anything interesting
to add, and there's nothing
to see, not here, not—
anyway.

II

"Perfect skin..." the old man doesn't seem interesting in
talking... "Can someone close the windows?" Walter is not
surprised... "The helicopter is for us..." As per our arrangement,
everything is for me... "Sometimes there are clouds..." A fleet
of vechiles shall arrive soon I think my ex-wife will see me
on television... "Darkness really is a special thing as far as
beauty is..." An awkward thought, but there's no going back...
"Someone please get the windows..." My ex-wife will think
something or she will not... "Oh, okay, Mr. Vegas has gone
inside already."

III

Dishes break into the house
This is how we await fireballs
    this old man told me darkness
    babies mewling in cribs abandoned
    mouths break into teeth
    the dust in the desert is born of bone

IV

THIS IS SOMEONE'S REVELATION
say something walter
anything, just once, while the driveways outside fill
"we're going
to be on the news"

b
l
a
ck

subspecies of category
I want to hold this girl before we maim her
look into her eyes
but that's not what
catharsis razorburn
"now here's an interesting pair of eyes"
I brought roses to my wife
when she said goodbye, and I didn't know it was coming
WALTER'S HANDS WON'T STOP SHAKING
fists perched atop thighs
presage orchids dressed in his memory

V

Who is the man?
I produced a folder, removed pictures,
shuffled them.

These are all the girls who have disappeared
in the last sixty years
in the radius of _____
you may be responsible for their deaths

but that is not what I am here for
tears now, after I killed a girl once
felt nothing, this absence
of me,
for whom do I grieve?
I was aloof
a professional, but aloof
I should have gone fishing
built model cars with my hands
poison, I wanted poison
or what, I don't
or what, why
I don't
I can't look at the pictures
my fingers
look at the pictures
I can't
which of the accused
nobody is accused
I am here to bring us all to justice

VI

I have no recourse for this staged plan
Stages of mourning,
if you listen, listen
stages of denial
all of us are killers, murderers, thieves
look at me

      You must look
           skyward, they wait for terminal descent
           there is an explanation
           there is always an explanation
When they find slaughtered girls
in ditches
cold skin, disappeared fish eyes
this is how we drown

ARE YOU
listening,
listening
this is how we
DROWN
this is how we
      listen

and I must remember what I wanted out of life
and I must remember where I was supposed to be for dinner
and I must remember
black figures whos peak to us
whisper, "there is causation, and it is not about capture"

to whom shall we apprehend this
      listen
      I listened and trembled
      vigils forgotten on cathedral footsteps

mummies with cigars wreathed in cloven desire
mummies with hands tattooed upon torso ceasure
there are not enough tombs
the man said there are not enough tombs

we stand upon an earth touched by open skulls
storytellers, shamans with animals masks slung
images of things that have always mattered
one eyeblink descends
doors shudder against frames
pictured, graceful surrender upon cracking knees

listen
if you can remember how to die
whosever apologizes upon the throne
of brick walls slick with rain
shall never have to live in the village outside of Xanadu

This
is how I
feel nothing

THE BITTERNESS OF
CONCLUSIONS

CHORUS FOR THIEVES

Our submission to years trembles the fitful breeze
Bloodprints of the tremulous headlines
Torpid peace collapses the chorus of thieves

The lords of the innocent surrender to withered knees
Look yonder for the pale twilight of forgotten graves
Our submission to years trembles the fitful breeze

The labrythine crimes absolve fragments, disease
March the anarchists through purgatorial mountainslides
Torpid peace collapses the chorus of thieves

Those lamentations, those sailors, those erasured degrees
One million gold doubloons for the triumphal arch of Babylon
Our submission to years trembles the fitful breeze

Gods and damn the youths of wasted streets and needs
Electronic templar knights lick the vote of pregnant tombs
Torpid peace collapses the chorus of thieves

Laugh at the truth of sorrowful men in Christ's shattered bazaar
Populations have plugged the lines of nations
Our submission to years trembles the fitful breeze
Torpid peace collapses the chorus of thieves

EULOGY FOR
HALF-REMEMBERED SUNDAYS

This is yesterday and we think of crime
Perhaps you did it
Think of the moment
Conjecture:
"This town is beautiful…"
"Maybe they killed more…"
"I think they are Satanists…"
"Why are the killers famous now…"
Campfire stories, conversations
Sounds like a blowtorch
Blue fire
Imperfect lawns were mowed again
Nobody was able to cancel the summer carnival

THEMATIC RETIREMENT

you wonder why we can't say anything else
why this tiresome question
cracks into garage doors
security cameras should be implanted in our faces

one ditch filled with bones
maybe nobody did anything here
have you heard the story?
whispers and daydreams oh my

better to talk among ourselves
this sense of justice
tired now, everything has been said
we've massacred all the bards, hanged them

incisions the word into white screen
inventing languages, turns of phrase
hairdresses of the apocalypse dry-humping literature
there isn't a structure

(there isn't a structure)

PRAISE FOR VINCENZO BILOF

"Philosophical and self-aware, Vincenzo Bilof is the Pablo Neruda of horror-genre fiction writing a bonafide master of prose and versification, He probes familiar tropes in a way that, to my mind, no one has done before—or could hope to emulate. Bilof shows zombies and werewolves in the same respect Wordsworth showed wandering clouds. His books are always well-researched (without ever being turgid), violent (while still being intuitive of nature's austere beauty) and maintain a healthy vein of satire and humour throughout. One of my favorites…"

—Chris Kelso, author of *The Black Dog Eats the City*

"Vincenzo Bilof's writing is an awesome mixture of chilling narrative and state-of-the-art details and inventions. Once you've begun the book, it is impossible to put down—it is like inserting both fingers into a power socket while standing barefoot in a puddle of water."

—Seb Doubinsky, author of *Song of Synth*

"Vincenzo Bilof's writing is like being beaten to death in an alley by Samuel Delaney and Chuck Palanhiuk with Robert Bloch occasionally coming over to kick you in the nuts. His darkly funny and extremely gruesome style makes him one of my favorite authors of the horror genre."

—Konstantine Paradias, reviewer at *Albedo One*

"The truth is that if you don't read all of Bilof's books you won't really get to know the tortured, twisted soul that creates all of this most wonderfully deranged fiction. A true master of the written and printed word."

—Jim Dodge, editor at *Zero Signal Magazine*